The Travels of Freddie and Frannie Frog

By Betsy Maestro
Illustrated by Giulio Maestro

A GOLDEN BOOK • NEW YORK

Western Publishing Company, Inc., Racine, Wisconsin 53404

Freddie and Frannie sat by the water's edge in their quiet cove. Frannie was reading a book about Christopher Columbus to her brother.

"Being an explorer is so exciting," said Frannie. "Maybe we could be explorers, too."

"What can we explore?" asked Freddie.

"The big pond," replied Frannie. "We've never been out there before."

"Can we leave now?" asked Freddie.

"First we have to build a boat," said Frannie.

So they began to build a boat. They used twigs
and sticks and bark. A lily pad made a great sail.
At last the boat was finished.

"It looks terrific," said Freddie. "But will it
float?"

"Of course!" said Frannie. She got into the boat and paddled around in a big circle. "See, I told you. We can leave first thing in the morning."

That night, Freddie and Frannie packed the things they would need for the trip.

The next morning, they set sail.

"Good-bye," called Mother. "Make sure you're home in time for dinner."

"Christopher Columbus didn't have to be home in time for dinner," complained Frannie.

"Well, you do," said Mother. "Have fun! Be careful!"

The wind blew and the boat sailed ahead on the sparkling water. "This was a super idea!" said Freddie to his sister.

Soon Frannie said, "Time to get to work."

"Aye, aye, Captain!" said Freddie.

"You write down everything that happens," said Frannie, handing her brother a logbook. "I'm going to make a map of the big pond. This is an important journey. You never know what we'll find."

Just then, the boat began to rock up and down.
Waves splashed up the sides.

"Look out!" shouted Freddie. "Here comes a
tidal wave."

A large wave washed over the boat.

"We're soaked," cried Freddie. "I'm glad the
boat didn't sink."

But Frannie said calmly, "Explorers just have to get used to tidal waves."

"Exploring sure makes me hungry," said Freddie. "Let's eat!"

Freddie and Frannie munched happily on sandwiches and cookies. They drank water from their canteens.

Suddenly Freddie saw a big shadow zooming
past. "What was that?" he shouted.

"I didn't see anything," said Frannie.

Then she looked up and saw a large bird. It was
getting ready to swoop down on them!

"Watch out!" Frannie cried.

Luckily, Freddie and Frannie managed to hide in some bushes nearby.

"Whew!" Freddie sighed. "That huge seabird almost grabbed us!"

"Explorers have to be very brave," said Frannie. "Christopher Columbus wasn't afraid of huge seabirds."

As the explorers sailed on, the gentle motion of the boat rocked them. They were just falling asleep when something hit the boat hard.

Bump! Bump! The boat shook.

Freddie looked over the side and saw two big eyes and a huge mouth. He jumped back.

Frannie grabbed a paddle and hit the thing over the head.

"Let's get out of here!" Freddie shouted.

They paddled away fast.

"Thank goodness you hit that monster," said
Freddie. "I think it was about to eat us!"

"It was only a giant sea creature, silly," said
Frannie. "Explorers meet up with giant sea creatures
all the time."

"I hope the rest of the trip will be more
peaceful," said Freddie.

As Frannie drew her map and Freddie wrote in his logbook, the boat drifted closer to shore.

Freddie and Frannie heard loud shouts, and saw two long sticks pointed at the boat.

"Those natives are going to spear us!" cried Freddie.

"Quick, into the water!" yelled Frannie.
They slid under the boat and waited. After a few
bumps and bangs, all was quiet again.
When Freddie and Frannie looked out, the
natives were gone.

Back in the boat, Frannie said, "It's almost dinnertime. We'd better head home."

Frannie put the finishing touches on her map. Freddie closed his logbook. As the boat neared the quiet cove, they could see their mother waving.

The next day, Freddie and Frannie went back to their favorite spot by the water. Frannie's new book was about the Wright brothers.

"It sure would be fun to fly," she said.

"Fly? We don't have an airplane," said Freddie.